W9-CFH-580

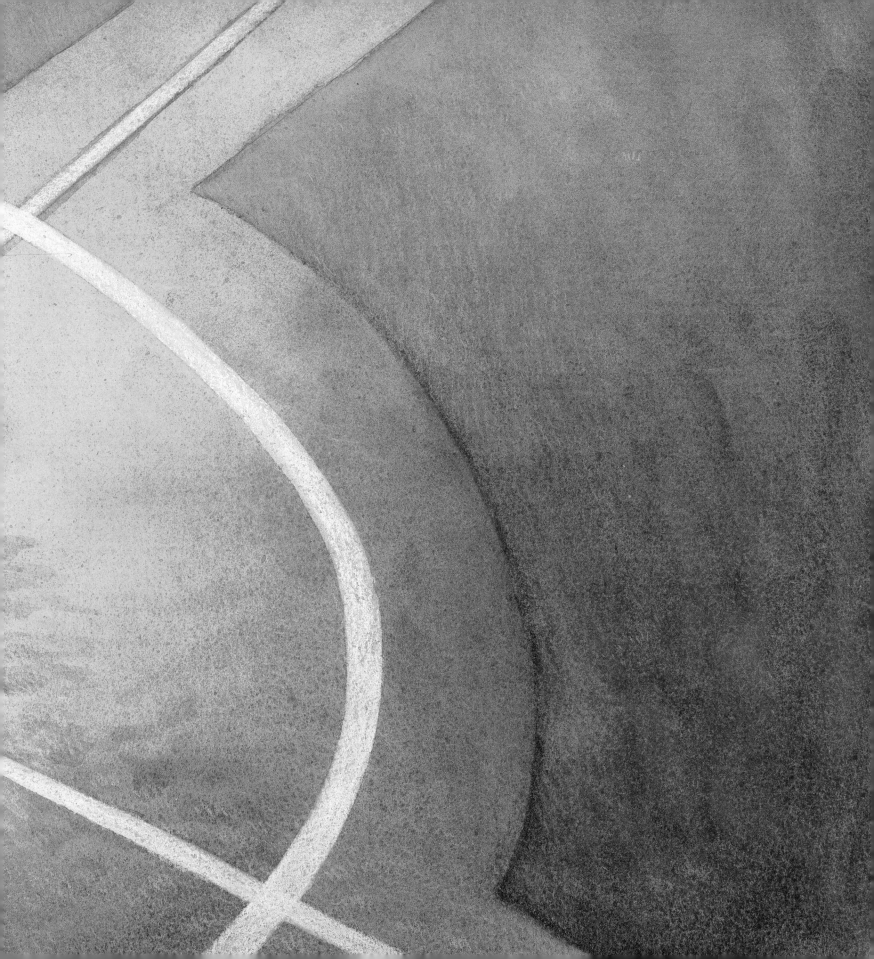

Take me out to the Ballgame

ALADDIN PAPERBACKS

Take me out to the Ballgame

illustrations by ALEC GILLMAN
original lyrics by JACK NORWORTH

BROOKLYN
DODGERS
NATIONAL
LEAGUE
CHAMPIONS

To the faithful fans from Brooklyn,
wherever they may be

—A.G.

to the ball game,

Take me out

with the crowd

Buy me some peanuts

and Cracker Jack,

Let me root,

root, root

for the home team,

If they don't win

it's a shame

For it's one,

two,

three strikes, you're out,

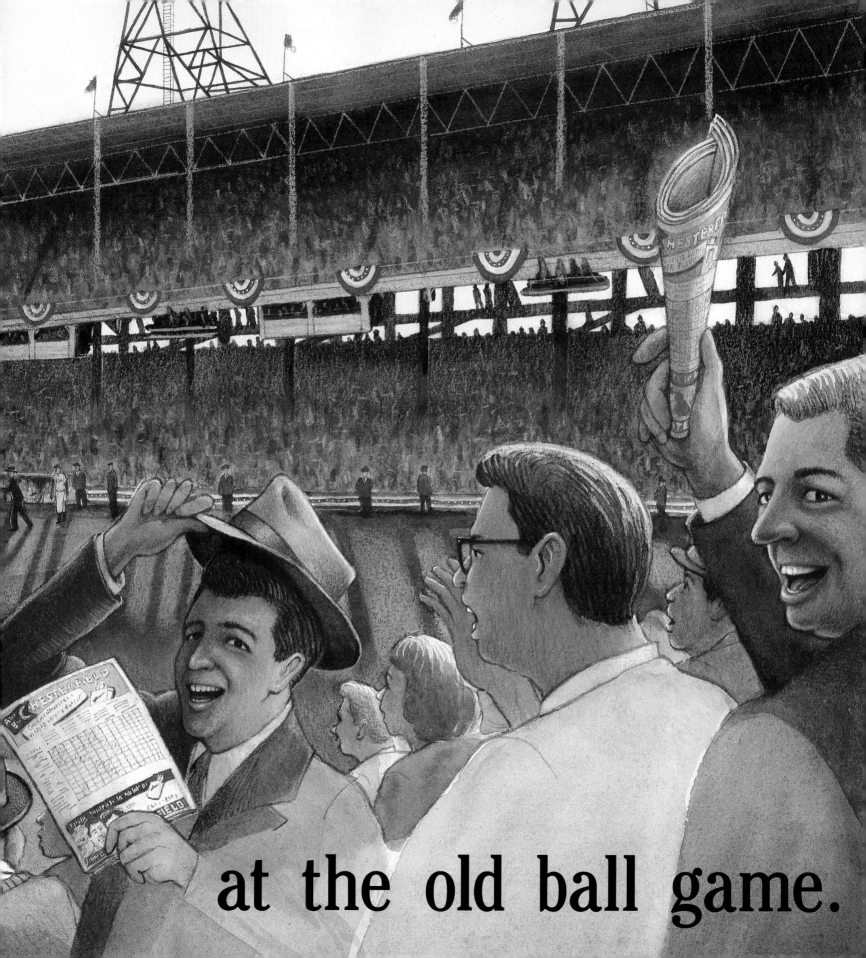

at the old ball game.

About

Take me out to the Ballgame

JACK NORWORTH

The Song

Jack Norworth (1879–1959), was born in Philadelphia, Pennsylvania. His father was an organ builder and choirmaster. Jack Norworth left home to join a minstrel show, and he soon became a popular song-and-dance man, headlining vaudeville stages for twenty years. From 1907 to 1913 he and his wife, Nora Bayes, performed together on Broadway and in vaudeville. Audiences loved their popular number, "Shine On Harvest Moon." Mr. Norworth also wrote songs for the Ziegfeld Follies and counted among his friends W. C. Fields.

It has been said that Jack Norworth, who had never been to a major league baseball game, wrote the lyrics to "Take Me Out To The Ball Game" during a short ride on the New York City subway in 1908.

Albert Von Tilzer (1878–1956), was born in Indianapolis, Indiana. A self-taught pianist, Albert Von Tilzer moved to New York City in 1900, where he worked in vaudeville and in the music publishing business. Mr. Von Tilzer also wrote songs for Broadway, and he contributed to several Hollywood movies, including *Birth of a Nation* (1930), *Here Comes the Band* (1935), and *Rawhide* (1938).

Albert Von Tilzer, who had also never been to a major league baseball game, wrote the music for "Take Me Out To The Ball Game" in 1908.

The Original Verses

Katie Casey was baseball mad,
Had the fever and had it bad;
Just to root for the home town crew,
ev'ry sou Katie blew
On a Saturday, her young beau
called to see if she'd like to go,
To see a show but Miss Katie said "no,
I'll tell you what you can do:"

Katie Casey saw all the games,
Knew the players by their first names;
Told the umpire he was wrong,
all along good and strong
When the score was just two to two,
Katie Casey knew what to do,
Just to cheer up the boys she knew,
She made the gang sing this song:

TAKE ME OUT TO THE BALL GAME

Jack Norworth

Albert Von Tilzer
Arr. David Wolff

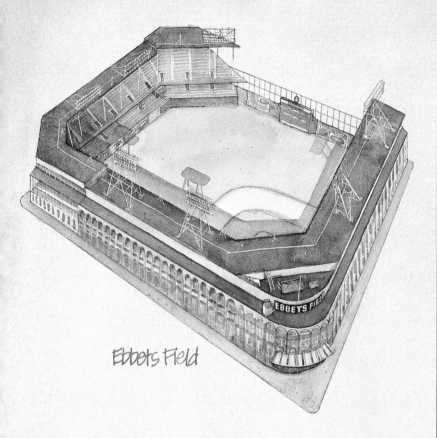

Ebbets Field

The Dream

I went to school in Brooklyn, New York, and I was able to see the various neighborhoods and public places that Brooklyn is famous for: Prospect Park, Coney Island, Atlantic Avenue, Flatbush, the Brooklyn Botanical Gardens, and the Brooklyn Museum, to name a few. The most elusive monument, however, was Ebbets Field, home to the Brooklyn Dodgers, and though it isn't standing anymore, memories of it linger among the many baseball fans who remember it best.

When I visited the site of Ebbets Field after talking with some of those fans, being immersed in photographs and footage of the park, and after reading about those Brooklyn Dodger days, I stood there, amazed, on the corner of McKeever and Sullivan places. It seemed as if the whole ballpark had just up and vanished....Indeed, I was too late, the Dodgers had left for Los Angeles in 1958. What I had read about, what I had pictured in my mind, what had seemed so very real to me as I painted the illustrations in this book, had been demolished in 1960, years ago.

How 'bout 'dem Bums?

For those who called Brooklyn home, Ebbets Field represented the hope that if this year wasn't so good, next year would be better. At Ebbets Field, there was always next year.

Amateur baseball in Brooklyn dates back to 1854, but it wasn't until 1884 that the professional Trolley Dodgers came to be. The team took its name from the close proximity of the streetcar junction to the field...daring spectators "dodged" trolleys on their way to a game. In 1913 Charles Ebbets built a new ballpark for his team a few blocks over from Flatbush, in Crown Heights. Along with Coney Island, it became a favorite gathering place in Brooklyn. A fan of the affectionately tagged "Bums" was usually loud, boisterous, and extremely loyal.

Only at Ebbets Field did the fans gain as much notoriety as the players. One such fan was Hilda Chester, who sat diligently out in the center-field stands, with clanging cowbell in hand. She sometimes led snake dances up and down the aisles in honor of the Dodgers and the town she loved best, Brooklyn. The Dodger Sym-Phony, composed of five or so musically disinclined fans from the nearby neighborhoods Williamsburg and Greenpoint, was often led by Shorty Laurice, accompanied by his friend Jocko. During the game they heckled the umpires with "Three Blind Mice" and taunted opposing players with "The Worms Crawl in, the Worms Crawl out."

Summer afternoons on the city streets were not complete without the smooth voice of Red Barber calling the game for radio. Red Barber announced for the Dodgers, from what he called his "catbird seat," from 1939 to 1953.

The Game

The 1947 World Series—besides being one of the most exciting contests in Series history—was the first to be televised, so it naturally brought the first $2 million gate. It was also the first to use six umpires. But most important to major league baseball were appearances by Jackie Robinson and Dan Bankhead, the first African-Americans to play in a World Series. The series also brought the eleventh world championship to the Yankees and sent the Brooklyn Dodgers, once more, into despair.

It had been six years since the Dodgers had made it to the series. In 1941 they had also challenged their arch-rivals, the "Bronx Bombers," the New York Yankees. Many Brooklyn fans remembered the day when victory seemed theirs. Then Dodger fireman Hugh Casey's third strike got away from catcher Mickey Owen, and Yankee Tommy Henrich made it safely to first, unleashing the subsequent winning runs. Brooklyn hadn't been the same since.

Many of the players in the 1941 Series returned to play in 1947—Joe DiMaggio, Tommy Henrich, and Phil Rizzuto for the Yankees, and from Brooklyn, Pee Wee Reese, "Pistol" Pete Reiser, Hugh Casey, "The People's Cherce (Choice)," Dixie Walker, and Cookie Lavagetto.

The Dodgers played miserably for the first three games; in fact they played like bums, dropping catches, swinging feebly at the ball, and losing the first two at Yankee Stadium, where shadows, distances, and cigarette smoke were supposed to make enemy outfielders giddy in the head. The Dodgers won the third game, though, back at Ebbets Field, despite Yogi Berra's pinch home run, the first in a World Series.

Game 4 looked like another Series first, a no-hitter going into the ninth inning. The Yankee pitcher, Floyd "Bill" Bevens, despite walking ten and scoring one on walks and a sacrifice, had kept the Dodgers hitless. With two men on base and two out, the loudspeaker blared, "Lavagetto batting for Stanky." The eleven-year Dodger veteran had been benched for most of this, his last season, replaced at third base by Spider Jorgensen. Cookie rubbed dirt on his hands and stepped up to the plate. The first pitch, he swung at viciously, missing. The next pitch was high, but when Cookie swung, he connected, sending the ball over right fielder Henrich's head and off the wall for a double. It was the only ball he hit right all year, and as the two runners scored, all of Brooklyn rejoiced.

From that moment the improbable became possible, the unpredictable Dodgers had a chance. The next day, Saturday, October 4, in Game 5, the Dodgers again found themselves—as the pictures in this book show—at Ebbets Field. And they found themselves in another fix, as Yankee pitcher Spec Shea threw the kind of game he was capable of and Joe DiMaggio smacked his second series homer. Dodger Jackie Robinson, wearing number 42, doubled, scoring one, but the Yankees were leading 2-1 in the bottom of the ninth.

The Dodgers had two out and the tying run on second as they tried to make lightning strike twice, sending Cookie up again to pinch-hit. But Yankee pitcher Spec Shea loaded the count, and then he threw a change of pace. Cookie swung…and missed. Now the Yankees were in the lead, three games to two, as the series headed back to the dreaded Yankee Stadium.

Game 6 was the longest 9-inning game—3 hours and 19 minutes—in Series history, and the Yankees used the most regular players (21) and pitchers (10) ever in a World Series game. But the Yankees lost, hustled to distraction by their irreverent visitors. Short but fleet-footed Al Gionfriddo, placed in left field for the Dodgers, raced toward the bullpen after Joe DiMaggio's potential 415-foot, 3-run homer, snatching it from the air with the very tips of his leathery fingers. The deafening screams from Dodger and Yankee fans alike could have stopped traffic three miles away. The series was tied.

Could it be possible after all those years of torment? Would the Dodgers finally achieve complete victory? Fans making the long subway trip back to Brooklyn could not help but dream of the next day's celebration. But in Game 7 Yankee pitcher Joe Page sealed the Dodgers' fate, blazing his fastball across the corners of the plate, allowing only one Dodger to reach base. The Dodgers trooped sadly home, while disgruntled Brooklynites renewed faith in their team, exclaiming, "Wait till next year."

COOKIE LAVAGETTO, after hitting his winning double, game 4 · 1947 World Series

The present day site of the former Ebbets Field

Selected Bibliography

The Baseball Encyclopedia. 8th ed. New York: Macmillan, 1990.

Drasnin, Irv (producer). *Forever Baseball.* Boston: WGBH Educational Foundation; Los Angeles: KCET; New York: WNET, 1989. (*Forever Baseball* first aired on November 7, 1989, as part of the PBS series, "The American Experience.")

Golenbock, Peter. *Bums: An Oral History of the Brooklyn Dodgers.* New York: G. P. Putnam's Sons, 1984.

Hitchcock, H. Wiley, and Stanley Sadie, eds. *The New Grove Dictionary of American Music.* London: Macmillan Press Limited, 1986.

Honig, Donald. *The Brooklyn Dodgers: An Illustrated Tribute.* New York: St. Martin's Press, 1981.

Norworth, Jack, and Albert Von Tilzer. *Take Me Out To The Ball Game.* New York: New York Music Co., 1908.

Smith, Robert. *World Series: The Games and the Players.* Garden City, New York: Doubleday, 1967.

The illustrations in this book were first drawn with pen and ink, then painted with watercolor, and finally highlighted with color pencil, in order to achieve a certain depth and realistic quality. I like to use heavyweight, cold press paper, so that I can soak the paper without having it wrinkle or buckle too much. The finished paintings were color-separated and printed using four-color process.

I would like to thank the knowledgeable staffs at the National Baseball Library at the National Baseball Hall of Fame in Cooperstown, New York; the Brooklyn Historical Society; and the Brooklyn Public Library.

First Aladdin Paperbacks edition March 1999
Aladdin Paperbacks • An imprint of Simon & Schuster Children's Publishing Division • 1230 Avenue of the Americas, New York, NY 10020 • Presentation, illustrations, and additional material copyright © 1993 by Alec Gillman • Arrangement copyright © 1993 by David Wolff • All rights reserved, including the right of reproduction in whole or in part in any form. • The publisher thanks Barbara Lalicki and Julie Quan. • The text for this book was set in Cheltenham Book Condensed. • Typography by Christy Hale • Printed in Hong Kong • 10 9 8 7 6 5 4 3 2

The Library of Congress has cataloged the hardcover edition as follows: Norworth, Jack. Take me out to the ball game / Alec Gillman ; illustrated by Alec Gillman ; with words from the old favorite, Take me out to the ball game, by Jack Norworth. — 1st ed.   p.   cm.
Summary: The lyrics of the familiar song, illustrated by pictures based on the World Series game played between the Dodgers and the Yankees in 1947 in Ebbets Field. ISBN 0-02-735991-3 (hc.)
1. Children's songs—Texts. [1. Baseball—Songs and music. 2. Songs.] I. Gillman, Alec, ill. II. Title. PZ8.3.N855Tak   1993   811'.54-dc20   91-18555
ISBN 0-689-82433-5 (pbk.)